W9-CLZ-146

Syracuse University

RESOURCE CENTER
HUNTINGTON HALL
Syracuse University

Wish Me Well

By John Ryckman and John McInnes

Drawings by Carl and Mary Hauge

GARRARD PUBLISHING COMPANY
CHAMPAIGN, ILLINOIS

Text copyright © 1971 by Thomas Nelson & Sons (Canada), Limited   Pictures copyright © 1971 by Carl and Mary Hauge
All rights reserved. Manufactured in the U.S.A.   Standard Book Number: 8116—6714—6
Library of Congress Catalog Card Number: 72—157848

Wish Me Well

One day Bunny Rabbit
went to see
Rick Raccoon.
"Rick," she asked,
"will you come out
and play with me?"

"Bunny," said Rick,
"I can't come out
and play with you.
I've been very sick,
and I must stay in bed."

"Oh, I'm sorry!" said Bunny.
"I wish I could help.
I'll go and ask
Fred the red squirrel.
He'll know what to do."

Bunny went to find
Fred the red squirrel.
Before long she came
to his house.
Fred opened the door.

"Hello, Bunny Rabbit,"
he said.
"Did you come
to play with me?"

"Oh no," said Bunny.
"I've come to ask for help.
Rick is very sick.
What can we do
to help him?"
"We'll go and look
for the Wishing Well,"
said Fred the red squirrel.
"We must hurry
and make a wish.
We want to wish
that Rick
will get well,"
said Fred.

Bunny and Fred started off
to find the well.
They looked and looked,
but they couldn't find it.

"Oh dear," said Bunny.
"Now Rick
will never get better."
The two friends
were very sad.
They sat down
and cried and cried.

It wasn't long
before Hopover the frog
came by.
"Hello," he said.
"Why are you sad?
Come along
and play with me."

"We can't play now,"
said Fred.
"We are looking
for the Wishing Well.
We can't find it."
"Rick the raccoon
is sick in bed.

We want him
to get better,"
said Bunny.
"Could you help us
find the well?"

"Yes," said Hopover.
"Come along with me.
It's not far from here.
But we must look out
for Bad Wolf.
He lives near the well."
It didn't take
the three friends long
to find the Wishing Well.

When they got there,
they had a surprise.
Bad Wolf was at the well.

He didn't see them.
He was making a wish.
"Wishing Well," he shouted,
"I am Bad Wolf.
Give me a wish."

"Who's there?" asked the well.
"I can't hear you."
"I'm Bad Wolf,
and I want a wish."

"Jump up on me,"
the Wishing Well said.
"I can't hear very well."
The wolf jumped up
on the well and shouted,
"I'm Bad Wolf."

"Why are you here?"
asked the Wishing Well.
"I'm here to make a wish.
I want a rabbit, a squirrel,
and a frog to come here.
I want to eat them up."
"I am an old, old well.
I can't hear you,"
said the well.
"Tell me your wish
once again.
Are you wishing
for something good?"
"Yes, yes," shouted the wolf.

"I'm wishing for something
good to eat.
Now give me my wish."
"I can't hear you,"
said the well.
"Look way down
into the water
and tell me again.

Who are you?
What do you want?"
Bad Wolf showed his teeth.
He looked way down
into the well.

"I want to eat
a rabbit, a squirrel,
and a frog for lunch,"
he shouted.
"I want you to give me
a big surprise."
"That's better," said the well.

"You want a big surprise.
I will be glad
to give you that."
Just then
there was a big splash.
The well pulled the wolf
into the water.

"Help, help!" he cried.
"I can't get out.
Wishing Well! Wishing Well!
Please help me!"

"Will you run away from here
and never come back?"
asked the well.
"Yes, yes," said the wolf.
"Is that your only wish?"
asked the well.

"Oh yes," said the wolf.
"Then out you go,"
said the well.
Splash went the water.
Out of the well
came the wolf.
"Now run away from here.
Never come back again,"
said the well.
"I don't like
those who make bad wishes."
Away ran Bad Wolf.
The three friends
went up to the well.

Bunny Rabbit looked
into the water.
"I'm Bunny Rabbit," she said.
"I want to make a wish."
"Is your wish a good one?"
asked the well.

"Yes," said Bunny.
"I want to make
a good wish.
It's not for me.
It's for Rick the raccoon.
He's very sick
and couldn't come here.
Will you please
make him better?"

"Rick is a good raccoon,
and he's our friend,"
said Fred the red squirrel.

Splash, splash
went the water.
"Your wish is a good one,"
said the well.
"Rick will be better
very soon."

"Thank you, Wishing Well,"
said the three friends.

"Let's go to see Rick,"
said Hopover the frog.

The friends went
to Rick's house.
They opened the door
and went in.

"Hello, friends," called Rick.
"I have a surprise for you!
This morning
I was sick in bed.
Now I'm well."

"I know," said Bunny.
"The Wishing Well
made you better."
"We went to the well
and made a wish,"
said the frog.

"Thank you, friends," said Rick.
"I'll run and thank the well.
Come along with me.
Then we can play
in the woods."

So Bunny Rabbit,
Fred the red squirrel,
Hopover the frog,
and Rick the raccoon
went and thanked the well.
Then they played games
in the woods.